MW00963751

Murdick's Mackinaw Mystery

Sarviol Publishing
Copyright © Nick Rokicki and Joseph Kelley, 2015

All rights reserved.
Without limiting the rights under copyright reserved above, no part of this
publication may be reproduced, stored in
or introduced into a retrieval system, or transmitted in
any form or by any means (electronic, mechanical, photocopying, recording, or otherwise),
without the prior written permission
of the copyright holder.

ISBN: 978-1512081329

Special wholesale and re-sale rates are available. For more information,
please contact Deb Harvest at petethepopcorn@gmail.com

When purchasing this book, please consider purchasing
an additional copy to donate to your local library.

Murdick's Mackinaw Mystery

9/2017 Kids:
to the wines Kids:
Always
READ!.

The wines Kids:
MAC
LOVES
BOOKS!

Nick
R.K.
2017

WRITTEN BY: NICK ROKICKI AND JOSEPH KELLEY

ILLUSTRATED BY: RONALDO FLORENDO

On a mild Monday morning in Mackinaw City, Michigan, magic and mystery were in the air. The month was September and summer was moving to an end.

Grandpa Francis Murdick was pacing about the kitchen, preparing to make fudge— a family tradition in the Murdick home.

Suddenly, a brisk breeze blew through the kitchen, creating a whirlwind of a mess, which swept the recipes for fudge swiftly out the window!

"I believe a search party is in order!" exclaimed Grandma Marcella, moved by the unfolding scene.

Hearing the commotion in the kitchen, Papa John and Mama Marcia had gathered with their children, Carrie, Ryan and Aaron. Each family member set out to their favorite spot, pursuing the family heirlooms.

Meanwhile, high in the sky above the cabin, flew Mac the Mosquito. Mac was a very observant mosquito… and he saw a large figure creeping about the shadows of the woods. The mysterious menace was collecting the recipe cards! Mustering his muscles against the wind, Mac decided to follow the thief into the forest.

Speaking of skies, Papa John was roaming the lands of Dark Sky Park, the main spot for viewing stars, and occasionally, when the luck struck, the Northern Lights! Of course, on this early morning, the stars were not to be observed in the sky, but the waves still washed on the beaches of Lake Michigan. John searched in tall, wavy grass… and over the pebbles that dotted the sand… and even under the rickety wood that molded a walkway. But no recipes were to be found.

Mac the Mosquito hovered over the head of the man, suddenly swooping low. In his buzzy voice, Mac whispered, "Wilderness State Park is the location you'll find the recipes."

Northward, Grandma Marcella meandered around the historical McGulpin Point Lighthouse, which was made—not manufactured — in 1869! Grandma consistently came here when she needed to clear her thoughts, take a deep breath, and think of the multitude of men and women that settled here, ages prior.

What better place would there be to find the recipes? Grandma rummaged along the milky white fence running the perimeter of the property… under the picnic tables that visitors used for a leisurely lunch… the caretaker even allowed her inside, to peek around the steep, spiral staircase that led to the luminous light. But no recipes were to be found.

Without warning, a loud buzz filled the ears of Grandma, which was a common thing in Michigan. But this time it was different. Grandma thought she heard, in the buzzing, "Wilderness State Park is the location you'll find the recipes."

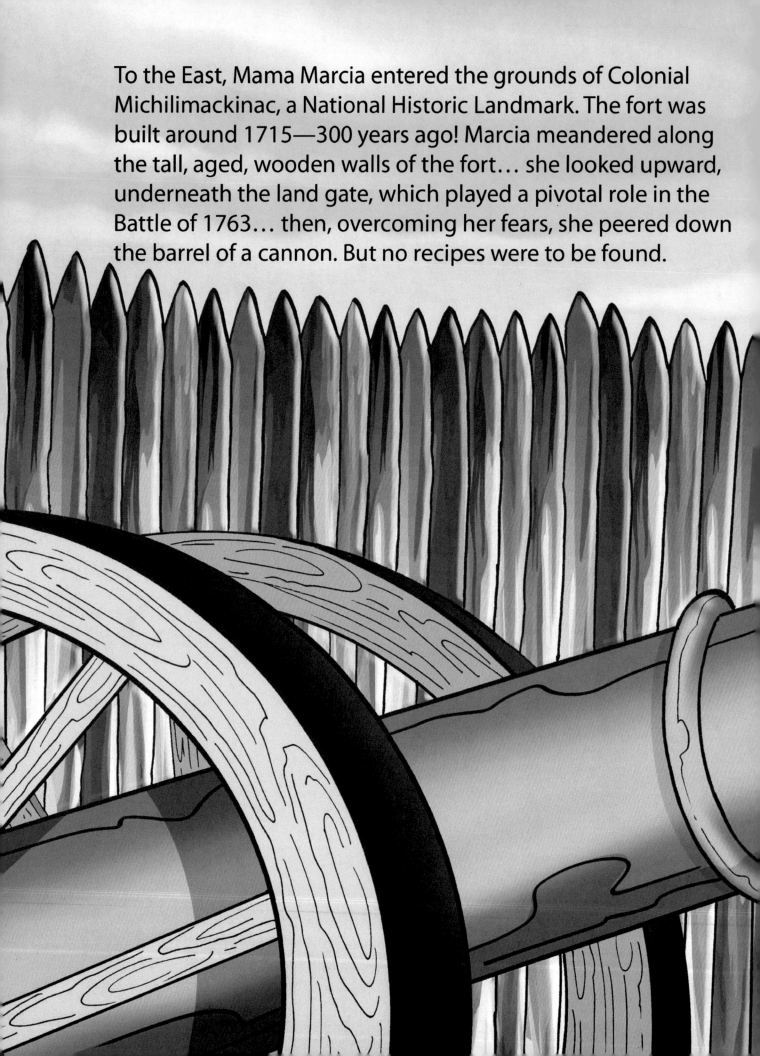

To the East, Mama Marcia entered the grounds of Colonial Michilimackinac, a National Historic Landmark. The fort was built around 1715—300 years ago! Marcia meandered along the tall, aged, wooden walls of the fort… she looked upward, underneath the land gate, which played a pivotal role in the Battle of 1763… then, overcoming her fears, she peered down the barrel of a cannon. But no recipes were to be found.

Marcia swatted at her ear as she heard a mosquito approaching. Luckily, she missed Mac the Mosquito by mere millimeters, as he sang, "Wilderness State Park is the location you'll find the recipes."

Carrie Murdick maundered the main boulevard of Mackinaw City, East Central Avenue. Marching between markets, she spotted an empty storefront. Carrie jumped up, getting a better look under the awning … she dug at the base of the tree in front of the shop … and she even pressed her forehead against the glass windows. She could see large slabs of marble. But no recipes were to be found.

Twisting, turning, spinning and oscillating in between the tourists visiting the Straits of Mackinac, Mac the Mosquito raced behind Carrie. Startled, she jumped as Mac whispered, "Wilderness State Park is the location you'll find the recipes."

Tiptoeing through the woods of Wilderness State Park, Ryan Murdick was careful to be on the lookout for wildlife. Black bear, beaver, bobcats, mink, muskrats and otter call the park home… he was the one visiting. Several years back, park rangers even spotted wolves pacing the peninsula! Ryan, being mindful not to disturb the foliage, heard a crackling sound behind him. Frightened to turn around quickly, he slowly pivoted to see his family standing behind him.

"What are you guys doing? Trying to scare the living daylights out of me?" mused Ryan.

"We all met up here! Something, or someone, was telling us to go to Wilderness State Park!" murmured Grandma Murdick. Sure enough, Grandma, Marcia and Carrie had all gathered.

"Wait! What's that noise?" moaned Marcia, a panicked look on her face. The members of the Murdick Family stood silent. Out of the shadows appeared a creature—a very large creature. A very large creature holding tiny, white cards.

Betty the Black Bear roared as she saw the family. After all, humans were the scariest thing that roamed the park!

"Go ahead, Betty! We talked about this—you've gotta be brave! You were keeping the recipes safe for the family, so return them!" Mac the Mosquito encouraged the bear.

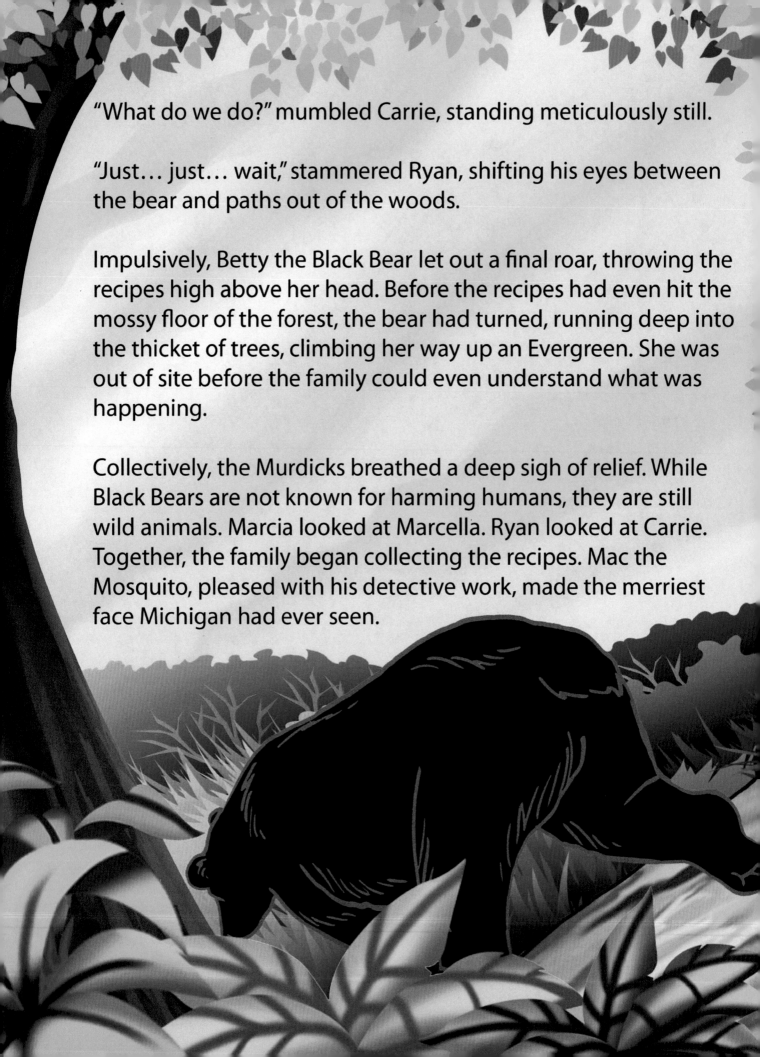

"What do we do?" mumbled Carrie, standing meticulously still.

"Just… just… wait," stammered Ryan, shifting his eyes between the bear and paths out of the woods.

Impulsively, Betty the Black Bear let out a final roar, throwing the recipes high above her head. Before the recipes had even hit the mossy floor of the forest, the bear had turned, running deep into the thicket of trees, climbing her way up an Evergreen. She was out of site before the family could even understand what was happening.

Collectively, the Murdicks breathed a deep sigh of relief. While Black Bears are not known for harming humans, they are still wild animals. Marcia looked at Marcella. Ryan looked at Carrie. Together, the family began collecting the recipes. Mac the Mosquito, pleased with his detective work, made the merriest face Michigan had ever seen.

In the meantime, back at the Murdick home, Grandpa Francis marched into the kitchen to a site that sent shivers down his spine. His grandson, Aaron, was pouring liquid fudge onto the marble slab in the kitchen.

"Aaron, what on Earth are you doing?" marveled Grandpa, his hands on his head.

"Grandpa, we don't need no stinkin' recipes! I've watched you make fudge since I was a baby! I've got it all right here," said Aaron, pointing to his head.

"No," said Grandpa, pressing his finger to Aaron's chest, "you've got it all right here."

Quietly witnessing the scene unfolding before them, the rest of the Murdick family stood at the doorway. In their hands, they held the recipes that brought all of them closer together.

"I guess fudge really is a family tradition, huh?" mentioned Ryan.

"Actually, Grandma… you've always taught us to share our talents with the world, no matter what sacrifices we have to make," said Carrie. "When I was searching for the recipes, I spotted an empty store downtown. Maybe we can all work together? And share our family talent?"

"Plenty of time for that, young lady. Right now, it's time to embark on a different family tradition—we gotta walk that bridge!" reminded Grandma Marcella.

Grandma was right. After all, this mild Monday morning in Mackinaw was Labor Day. And on every Labor Day for more than 50 years, Michiganders and Michiganders-at-heart walk across the Mighty Mac, the Mackinac Bridge… the span which connects two different worlds, the Upper and Lower Peninsulas of Michigan, the 26th State!

What types of traditions do you share with your family?

The History of Murdick's Fudge

The first Murdick's Fudge store was founded on Mackinac Island in 1887, the same year that the Grand Hotel opened. The Murdick family no longer owns the original fudge store on the island, but continues making their delicious fudge, taffy, brittles, and other candies in Mackinaw City, Frankenmuth, Charlevoix and Traverse City. The Murdicks are proud of their heritage and their customers say it's still the creamiest fudge to be found!

About our Product

Murdicks still use the same recipes that were handed down to them by family so many years ago. They cook their fudge in copper kettles, cool it on marble slabs, work it to a set, and slice it for the showcase as customers look on in awe. It is always fun for "fudgies" to watch the Murdicks work their magic and taste the creamy, smooth fudge while it is warm right off the slab!

Contact Us

Create your own family tradiiton by visiting us at our locations in Mackinaw City and Frankenmuth. For our readers across the country, orders for fudge may be placed online at www.AaronMurdicksFudge.com

Aaron Murdick's Fudge
219 E. Central Avenue
Mackinaw City, MI 49701

Toll Free Ordering
(844) 687-3425

© ANN TELICZAN
WWW.MICHIGANSWEETSPOT.COM

Francis, Aaron and John Murdick, three generations of candy makers. Today, the Murdicks carry on the family tradition, started in 1887.

72590405R00025

Made in the USA
Columbia, SC
21 June 2017